Date Du

THE RICE BOWL PET

THE RICE BOWL PET

By Patricia Miles Martin
Illustrated by Ezra Jack Keats

THOMAS Y. CROWELL COMPANY · NEW YORK

BY THE AUTHOR

The Little Brown Hen

The Rice Bowl Pet

Manufactured in the United States of America
Library of Congress Catalog Card No. 62-7744
4 5 6 7 8 9 10

THE RICE BOWL PET

AH JIM lived in Chinatown.

From the window of his apartment he could see balconies and roof tops. Over the roof tops the sea gulls swooped high in the sky above San Francisco Bay.

On the balconies of the houses his neighbors watered their plants and played with their pets. There was a woman with a red and gold parrot in a cage, and a man with a black cat on his shoulder. Ah Jim liked to watch the parrot and the cat.

He said to his mother one day, "I would like to have a pet." His mother was busy cooking. She didn't even look at him.

He said it three times before his mother answered.

"Our family is big and our apartment is small," she said. "There is not much room. But you may have a small pet. It must be little enough to fit in a rice bowl."

At supper, when Ah Jim ate his rice, he held his chopsticks carefully and did not spill a single grain. He looked at his rice bowl. It was very small.

"I don't know what pet I want," he said.

His brothers laughed at him.

"Do you want a turtle?" they asked. "Do you want a cricket?"

But Ah Jim didn't know.

After supper, his oldest brother said, "Forget about your pet. Come with us to the theater. You will like the play."

At the theater, Ah Jim watched. There were animals in the play, but they were only red dragons and yellow tigers, made of paper.

Paper animals were not much fun.

The next morning Ah Jim went to the American school. He was polite to everyone. He said his lessons for the teacher. He spoke English without an accent.

At noon he ate his lunch in the big schoolyard with his friends.

"Have you a pet?" he asked Ling Sam.

"I have a little turtle," said his friend.

"I have a cricket," said Ping Loo.

A turtle or a cricket would be small enough to fit in a rice bowl. But Ah Jim would have to keep the turtle in a glass jar, and the cricket in a bamboo cage. The turtle would not be free to crawl and the cricket would not be free to jump.

He knew that he didn't want a turtle or a cricket.

At the end of the day at the American school, Ah Jim went down the street to the Chinese school. He learned about the watch towers on the Great Wall of China. He learned about sampans on the Yellow River. He learned to read and write in Cantonese. He spoke Cantonese perfectly. Even his thoughts were in Cantonese.

What kind of a pet do I want? he thought. Do I want a grasshopper? Do I want a goldfish? No. A grasshopper would not be free to hop, and the fish could swim only in small circles.

When Saturday came, he looked at his rice bowl again. "I'll take it with me," he said, "and find a pet that will fit." He walked up the hill to the shops. Every shop had things to look at. In one window he saw a tiny jade elephant.

"There is a pet that would go in my rice bowl," he said. But he did not want a jade elephant. He wanted a live pet.

Through the window, he saw something run across the shop. It was a little dog, the littlest dog he had ever seen. It was the color of gold, with two eyes and a nose like three shining black buttons. It jumped into a small basket.

The dog would make a nice pet. It was almost what he wanted, but not quite.

It would not fit in the rice bowl.

As Ah Jim looked through the shop window, the glass felt cold and smooth against his nose. Two black-button eyes looked back at him from over the side of the basket.

The shopkeeper came outside.

"Do not press your face against my window," he said. "Boys and girls come to look at the dog in my shop, and I must always wash this window after they leave." He groaned loudly.

Ah Jim hurried away, carrying his empty bowl carefully.

After his lunch Ah Jim went out to play. He still carried his rice bowl.

At the top of the hill his brothers were flying their kites—kites that looked like giant golden butterflies. Ah Jim stopped to watch them.

He thought about the golden dog he had seen in the store. If only it were small enough to fit in his rice bowl!

"Look at our hungry brother," said the oldest brother. "He carries an empty rice bowl in his hand."

"He doesn't know what he wants to put in it," said the second brother.

"Why don't you go to a pet shop?" asked the third. "Maybe you'll see something little."

As Ah Jim was walking toward the pet shop, he met a boy from his school.

"What are you carrying?" asked Ah Jim.

"A frog," the boy said.

"Can I hold it?" Ah Jim asked.

The boy held Ah Jim's bowl, and Ah Jim held the frog. One minute the frog was in his hands, and the next minute it was gone.

It had hopped inside his shirt.

Ah Jim hopped too, while he reached for the frog.

I do not want a frog, he thought. It is too cold. I want a warm pet.

At the pet shop, he saw many animals: a big monkey swinging on a bar, a green parrot on a perch, a black cat with a silver bell around its neck. Then he saw two parakeets. They were small. Just the right size to go in a rice bowl.

Ah Jim looked at them. He did not want two parakeets. He wanted a pet he could hold.

On the way back to Chinatown, he thought of little things: worms, guppies, snails—

He decided to go to Fisherman's Wharf.

He climbed aboard a cable car and sat outside. On the turns, the gripman called in a loud voice:

"Watch out for the curve!"

Presidio Ave California
& Market
Streets

Ah Jim slid along the wooden seat and held tightly to his rice bowl.

"Why are you holding an empty rice bowl?" the conductor said.

Ah Jim did not know how to answer.

"What do you expect to put in it?" the conductor asked.

Ah Jim did not wish to say. He looked down at the rice bowl in his hands.

The people on the cable car laughed at him, but he did not laugh back. He wanted only to reach the end of the line.

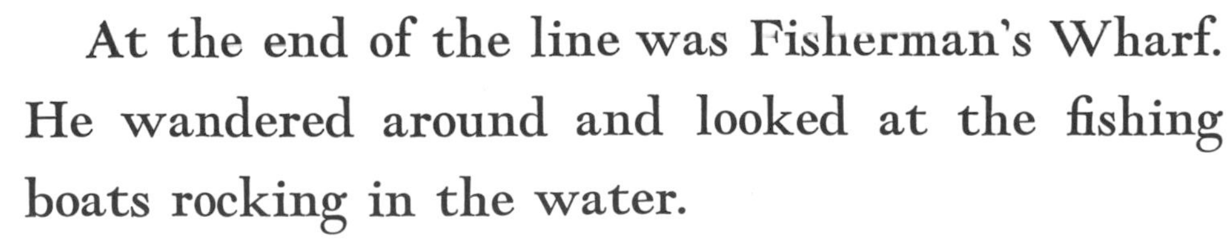

At the end of the line was Fisherman's Wharf. He wandered around and looked at the fishing boats rocking in the water.

He smelled the seafood cooking in the brick vats along the walk. He looked for a pet.

A crab is too large, he thought. A lobster is too

large. And even if they were small, they are not good pets, for they nip a finger unless you are careful.

He decided he did not want a crab or a lobster.

He wanted a pet he could hold, a pet that was warm, a pet that would fit in his rice bowl.

He could not forget the dog that was the color of gold, the dog that was almost little enough to fit in his rice bowl.

He rode back to Chinatown, and when at last he reached the shop with the jade elephant in the window, he stopped. The little dog was still there. Ah Jim pushed his face against the windowpane.

The shopkeeper came outside.

"*You* again," he said. He shook his head sadly. "You come to look through my window and so I do nothing but wash off finger and face marks all day long. Please go."

Ah Jim saw that the windowpane was covered with smudges. He turned and ran.

Around the corner, he stopped. He thought about all the fingermarks on the windowpane, the smudges he had made. He went back to the shop.

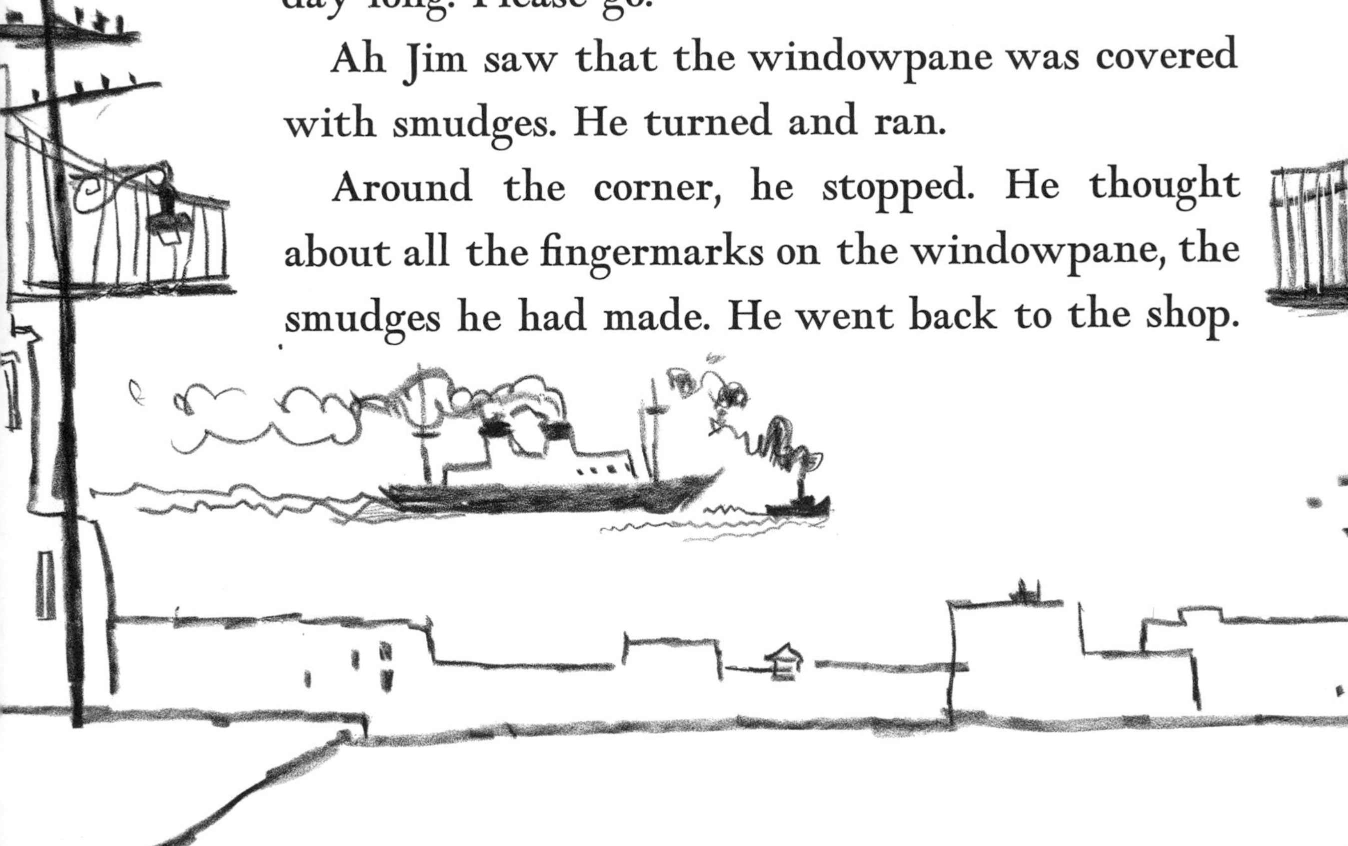

大

The shopkeeper was starting to wash the window and he scowled when he saw Ah Jim.

Ah Jim spoke quickly. "I would like to wash the window for you."

"But the marks here are not all *your* fingermarks," the shopkeeper said.

"I know," said Ah Jim, "but many are mine. I will wash the window."

"Very good," said the shopkeeper.

Ah Jim set his rice bowl down on the walk and started to work.

He cleaned and polished, watching the golden dog all the while. Then he cleaned and polished again.

When the window was shining bright, he looked inside the shop and saw the shopkeeper and his wife laughing there.

"Come in, come in," the shopkeeper called. "My wife and I have thought of a very good thing."

Ah Jim went inside.

"Tomorrow," the shopkeeper said, "the little dog goes back to China with our brother. Our brother leaves one puppy." He reached inside the small basket.

There in the shopkeeper's hand was the tiniest puppy Ah Jim had ever seen. The man handed it to him.

"Now," said the shopkeeper, "if you will take this puppy, there will be no reason for boys and girls to come to our window to press noses and hands against our clean glass, for the dogs will be gone."

The puppy was the color of gold.

It was warm.

And it was *just* the right size to fit into his rice bowl.

Ah Jim tried to thank the man, but no words came.

The woman smiled. "Do not speak," she said. "We see your thanks in your face."

Ah Jim walked down the street, carefully carrying the puppy in his rice bowl. Its bark, he knew, would be no louder than the sound of bamboo wind chimes hanging in a doorway.

He walked down the hill and up the stairs to his apartment.

"LOOK," he said. "It fits in my rice bowl."

His brothers laughed, and after a while, his mother laughed too.

And Ah Jim laughed the longest of all.

ABOUT THE AUTHOR

Patricia Miles Martin learned to ride horseback when she was five years old. Then she acquired a Saint Bernard dog and a succession of cats. Since that time her major interests in life have been animals and writing books for children. In *The Rice Bowl Pet* she has combined these two loves in a particularly satisfying story.

Mrs. Martin was born in Cherokee, Kansas. Now she and her husband live in San Mateo, California, in a farmhouse that is a perfect setting for the antique pressed glass and kerosene lamps that Mrs. Martin collects.

ABOUT THE ILLUSTRATOR

Ezra Jack Keats has traveled throughout Europe, Great Britain, Cuba, and the United States, painting everywhere he goes.

Mr. Keats was trained at the Art Students League and has taught art in New York City, where he lives. Now he spends most of his time illustrating children's books.